The Writer's Cats

ALSO BY

Muriel Barbery

The Elegance of the Hedgehog
Gourmet Rhapsody
The Life of Elves
A Strange Country
A Single Rose

Muriel Barbery

Illustrated by Maria Guitart

The Writer's Cats

Translated from the French by Alison Anderson

Europa
editions

Europa Editions
1 Penn Plaza, Suite 6282
New York, N.Y. 10019
www.europaeditions.com
info@europaeditions.com

Copyright © Éditions de l'Observatoire/Humensis,
Les chats de l'écrivaine, 2020
First publication 2021 by Europa Editions

Translation by Alison Anderson
Original title: *Les chats de l'écrivaine*
Translation copyright © 2021 by Europa Editions

Library of Congress Cataloging in Publication Data is available
ISBN: 978-1-60945-716-7

Illustrations © 2020 by Maria Guitart

Art direction and original book design, Studio Humensis

Further design by Emanuele Ragnisco
www.mekkanografici.com

To my Pepito
To Karole Armitage

To my family
To Matilda and Aleix,
stay wild and keep on smiling

First of all, let me make one thing clear: we like our writer. She's kind. She never forgets when it's time for our meal. She doesn't scream when she sees a dead mouse. She tosses bottle corks to us (our favorite game at aperitif time) while she's drinking wine (which is not infrequent). She takes us to the vet the minute we fart out of tune. We really do like her.

But enough is enough.

I'll tell you straight: without us, our writer would not be the writer she is. I don't know if she'd be worse or better, but she'd be different, that's all. Why? Because even if we can't speak, we are peerless literary advisors.

"How can a cat claim to be a literary advisor?" you might wonder (and rightfully so). I shall explain.

But first allow me to introduce our tribe. We are four Chartreux cats, which means we have gray fur and orange eyes. When our writer's best friend saw us for the first time, he said, "They go nicely with the walls."

We live in a house in the country, with taupe-gray walls, brown sofas, and orange cushions. At one end of the house there's the writer's study, at the other is her husband's music studio. From time to time, they meet in the middle, in other words in the kitchen, where the cupboards are gray and the dishtowels are orange.

I'm Kirin. I'm four years old. The others are my brother Petrus, then Ocha (a male) and Mizu (a female), who are four years older than Petrus and me and are also brother and sister. We come from the same breeder; Ocha and Mizu's father is one of our grandfathers—Petrus's and mine, that is. We get along well, we are from the same family, after all. But we each have a distinct personality and, I might add, very individual neuroses.

Ocha is the boss. Ocha means "tea" in Japanese. Our writer absolutely adores Japan. She used to live there. She goes back often. She gets a tremor in her voice when she talks about it. She drinks gallons of sencha (refined green tea). When she is pleased with her work, she treats herself to a little gyokuro (even more refined green tea). She has an impressive number of Japanese teapots, cups, and bowls, some to drink from, others to look at. Apparently, they are *wabi-sabi*, a Japanese concept used to describe a "humble, unassuming" esthetic. Personally, I find them rather grubby and I prefer English porcelain with gilt edges and pink butterflies, but that's a topic for another day.

Ocha is bigger and stronger than your average Chartreux, but he's a softie who purrs and meows like a kitten. Moreover, he's eight years old and it's been a long time since he went around chasing mice all day. He would rather snooze by the fire while waiting for dinner, and he'd kill brothers, sisters, musician, and writer for a mere crumb of pâté. Does this surprise you? It just so happens that Chartreux are known to be proper gourmands, so really, don't start reproaching us for our hedonism and our joie de vivre.

After Ocha in the pecking order comes his sister, Mizu. She was born with abnormalities, which have touched our writer's heart (moreover, in her novels there are always characters with abnormalities): Mizu's front legs are shorter and slightly twisted (in profile she looks like an inclined plane), she is smaller but also livelier, and walks like a ferret. Apparently cats like this are called munchkins. It's a genetic mutation that can occur in any breed. But evidently, it also gives her a particular aptitude for communicating with humans: our writer has endless discussions with her in the morning when she's at her desk with Mizu curled closely against her right hip.

Like Ocha, Mizu loves her food, but it is not her main preoccupation. The thing that Mizu hates most of all is when someone encroaches on her territory. Don't you dare put a paw on the sofa where she is snoring, or your pads on *her* section of the bench. Mizu is territorial, and she doesn't mess around when it comes to private property. If you have to go anywhere near her, make a large detour or else wave a little flag that says, I'm just passing through. The trade-off is that you can always count on her when times are hard. She's a strong cat, she can move mountains, and without her you would certainly not be reading these lines. Oh, and I nearly forgot: in Japanese, Mizu means "water," just in case you haven't caught the drift by now. The water for the tea, get it?

The third cat is my brother Petrus. As I said, we each have our own little neuroses but Petrus, in fact, is an exception. Not a single neurosis: Petrus is always happy. You feed him, he's happy. You don't feed him? He's happy, too. It's cold, it's hot, the door is closed, the door is open? No problem. Maybe it's due to his name, the name of one of our writer's characters—a very likable alcoholic elf character, who always looks on the bright side of life. Then there's Petrus the wine, get it? That may not be Japanese anymore, but it's still drinking. Having said that, Petrus may not have any neuroses, but he does have taste. You could even say he's the most refined cat of us all because what Petrus likes more than anything on earth is flowers.

He can spend hours sniffing the roses in the garden. He touches them gently with his paw. He rubs against them. He blows on them, gently. Sometimes he nibbles a little piece. Of course, all these things make our writer ecstatic: an entire section of her library is devoted to her books about flowers, so a cat that has a thing for lavender, just imagine! She can't get enough of encyclopedias full of wildflowers and herbal remedies, and ikebana (Japanese floral art), and now that she's living in the country, she takes meticulous care of her living flowers. Japan, a garden, a cat that's crazy about roses: you can see how consistent it all is.

And finally, there's me, Kirin. In case you didn't know, Kirin is a kind of Japanese beer. Still consistent. When they go to Japan, our writer and her husband drink a lot of beer (and a fair amount of sake too). That's one thing, but there's something else: I'm very pretty. One day a dear friend of our writer's said: this cat is so round and soft and gray, so charming, so graceful, her eyes are so orange, her whiskers so silky, she's my little Sunshine. Since that day they sometimes call me Sunshine, too, and I suffer from the syndrome of fatal beauty: what if, someday soon, they no longer think I'm that beautiful? What if tomorrow they lose interest in me?

Like every cat on earth, we spend our days hunting, sleeping, eating, and sleeping some more. We meow to go out, and once we are out, we meow to come back in. We turn our noses up at the litter tray and do our business where it will be in the way, in the middle of the gravel path (except for me, because I'm modest and prefer the discretion of the cellar, at the foot of the wine racks). We courteously deposit our dead mice on the parquet floor in the corridor that our masters go down in the middle of the night, in the dark, barefoot, on their way to the bathroom. We always sprawl in the very spot where they would like to sit or work. We shamelessly deny ever committing the least little crime, even when our noses are blatantly covered in jam.

In short, like every cat on earth, we would most happily spend the rest of our days in the house of the writer and the musician were it not for the fly in the ointment. Yes, you got it: in addition to being ordinary cats, we are authentic literary advisors and, as extraordinary as that might seem, this singular quality gives us rights. Kibble-induced serenity can be deceptive, it's how they put us to sleep, how they buy us. But we can no longer keep silent.

In the beginning, we wondered if we were somehow unique. All writers have cats who, as far as we know, have never claimed their due. So, we did some research. Our findings were indisputable: apart from Baudelaire's cat Tibère, who was suspected in his time of being more than a mere cat (but there was no definitive proof thereof), we have not found a single cat of our ilk in the body of works we consulted.

Armed with this certainty, we set out to find allies. Mizu convened an extraordinary counsel to decide on potential candidates.

There were three.

Our writer's long-time editor (the one who discovered her twenty years ago, then went on to become a very dear friend) is a smiling human with a mustache, known to be conscientious both in his work and in his assiduous appreciation of his authors' wine cellars. As he lives in the region, he comes here often, and we have had ample opportunity to make his acquaintance. At first glance, he would seem to be the ideal candidate: no one knows the nature of a writer's work better than he does. In addition, he's a very funny man, of the biting-but-kindly-ironic sort, who can make me meow with laughter. *Last but not least*, as chic French people like to say (in English), he's a *bon vivant* (the Rabelaisian variety), and an excellent chef, and so our writer regularly turns to him for her mayonnaise—mayonnaise fit for hedonists, I might add, having once or twice dipped my nose (carelessly) into it. Given all this (*mens sana in corpore sano*), you might think that we'd found our man.

Alas! The editor has not manifested the slightest degree of either interest or empathy where cats are concerned. Our writer's besotted love for us, her earnest efforts to speak to us as if we were creatures blessed with the gift of speech, leave him baffled—a bafflement that is quickly drowned, it is true, in a glass of Vouvray, but we must face facts: in his eyes we are merely an accumulation of furry molecules, and he will never lift even his little finger for us.

Of course, there is also our writer's husband. He is even more familiar with the daily nature of her work than her editor is. But no matter how greatly we believe in the legitimacy of our cause, we are not, for all that, impervious to compassion. The writer's husband already has to put up with the writer. This is a full-time job, interspersed with bursts of foul temper and tirades full of bad faith for the sole reason (never admitted to) that she is displeased with how her work has gone that morning. You'd have to hear some of their conversation to believe it, then wonder why he doesn't slam the door in the face of his beloved pain in the ass. No, honestly, if Stoicism had a face, it would be his, and we cannot, on top of everything else, ask him to embrace our fight.

MIAOU!

And then there is Minou. Minou is
a writer, and a friend of our own writer.
Minou is a defender of animal rights.
Minou has a Noah's Ark in the countryside
near where we live, with animals of all kinds, including a naked (pink) cat, a pig, a Spanish Galgo (the size of a pony)
and dwarf sheep. Minou is vegan. Minou comes to look after us
when our masters go to Japan (except when he is there himself).
Unlike the editor (who is also his editor), Minou is crazy about
cats. And that is why our writer gave him the nickname Minou,
which in French means, simply, Kitty.

Yes, Minou is a nice guy. Unfortunately, he's rather limited. No matter how often and loudly I meow our request at him, he gives me a stupid smile in return and says, "What a sweetie this one is, and talkative on top of it"—in short, Minou may be a defender of animal rights, but he takes us for simple four-legged creatures, and there is about as much chance that he'll rally to our cause as for Ocha to turn his nose up at a rancid old piece of kibble forgotten behind a bowl.

"Will we ever get to the point?" you must be wondering at this stage in the story. And you have every right to wonder, I'll grant you that, so I shall try to set the scene. Our writer works at a little desk in a little study off of the living room. Before Petrus and I were born, she used to settle into a comfortable chair, and Ocha and Mizu would go and lie down on either side of her notebook. When we came along, the desk was too small for the four of us, so she acquired a little bench where three can fit nicely (I mean one human and two cats). As a rule, Mizu sprawls first, next to her right hip, followed by one of us on her left, and the other two take up their position on the desk. Note her intention: our writer actually *bought* this little bench so that we could stay by her side while she was working.

On Judgment Day, no one will be able to plead innocence.

Our writer wakes up early, between five and six in the morning, and works until her musician gets up, rarely before nine, and rarely very chipper. Moreover, during breakfast, whether he wants to or not, he is awarded the privilege of hearing the exhaustive summary of the morning's writing. Over the years he has learned to nod his head with conviction while thinking about other things, but it doesn't always work. When this happens, our writer loses her temper and breakfast really starts going downhill for the musician, who wanted nothing more than a little peace and quiet on Planet Earth. Still, the major difference between our writer's husband and us is that he isn't there *while* she is writing. Otherwise, he would know why we are hopping mad and ready to jump ship.

Enough is enough, as I said once already.

For a start, you have no idea how difficult a writer's work can be. There are days when our writer sits drinking tea with Minou, and she moans, "I'll never manage." And Minou, in unison, "Neither will I." Then they feel sorry for each other while consuming three or four pots of tea, then Minou goes away looking glum, and our writer glances over at us, looking morose. So, we know very well how difficult it must be. And what's more, we know why, because she says the same thing to her husband every morning: if only all I had to do was tell a story, it would be easy.

"So, what else does a writer have to do?" you might wonder. Well, write. Which means working on your (a formidable word, full of doubt and desire) *language*. Worse yet (laden with restless terror) on one's *style*. And all of it with *poetry* (the very gates of hell). Writers are hypocrites who would love to tell a good yarn the way your old Uncle Marcel used to, but they feel compelled to cloak their story with all sorts of flowery and complicated turns of phrase like that other Marcel. Which isn't easy, I have to admit, and this explains why writers suffer from three afflictions.

The first is restlessness. There are mornings when our writer mumbles, squirms on her seat, stands up, sits down, starts writing again with multiple displays of grunting and crossing out, then she starts the whole rigmarole again before hurling her pen on the table in a rage. That is when we come on stage: Mizu squeezes against her right hip, Ocha snuggles on her left and purrs, Petrus takes up his position next to her free hand, and I stretch gracefully at the top of her notebook, looking her in the eyes, gently moving my tail, then (coup de grâce) grazing her wrist with the pads of my paws. She caresses me distractedly, scratches Petrus's spine, murmurs, "My Mizu," then, fiddling with Ocha's ear, "Beautiful cat," and, in the end, the world is back in place: all is calm, pacified, right side up again. She picks up her pen, meditates for a moment, swoops back down on her page, and works peacefully until her musician wakes up.

The second writer's affliction is doubt. In reality, writing and doubt are two facets of the same art. This is one of their favorite topics, when she's with Minou: the growth of doubt, the amplification of doubt, the frenetic cavalcade of doubt, and even, no less, doubt as their cross to bear. It occupies them for at least two whole teapots, until they come to their customary lamentations about how it's obvious they'll never manage (two more teapots). The writer is a perverse creature who has chosen an impossible trade, a calling that will doom her (or him) to dissatisfaction for all eternity, when all she dreams of is nothing more than finishing her crossword while she sips her drink. I'll tell you straight: calming our writer's restlessness is one thing, but confronting her doubt is another kettle of fish. There was no way around it, we had to resort to a certain necessary evil.

We learned how to read.

"Learned how to read!" you say, astonished. It wasn't that difficult: our writer often reads her texts out loud, and all Mizu had to do (because she's a clever kitty) was peer at the page at the same time. Then she taught all three of us, Ocha, Petrus, and me—and she was not a fun teacher, either, she gave us homework for the next day and would mete out punishments from some bygone era (including the dunce's cap). But the fact remains that now we know how to read and decipher our writer's (terrible) handwriting, although, as a rule, we wait for her to type up the day's text on the computer, print it out, and set it meticulously in the middle of her desk to be reread the following morning. And so, during the night, while she is trapped in the tormented slumber of the writer who wonders what her prose will look like at first morning light, we read.

Mizu takes the pages in her fangs one after the other, and we read conscientiously. Then we confer. We really enjoy these discussions about the text, which lead to fascinating altercations. For example, unsurprisingly, Ocha is captivated by dinner scenes, Mizu likes battle scenes best of all, Petrus is crazy about descriptions where there are flowers, and I like the love stories. But we are also capable of objectivity. Once we have all shared our preferences, we turn our attention to consistency, relevance, and the narrative progression of the text. Language and style. And on this we almost always agree. Is it because we are Chartreux cats in a world of gray walls and Japanese orange lacquer vases? It could be yet another question of consistency.

After the diagnosis, it's time for action. The following morning, when our writer is rereading the work she did the day before, Mizu sprawls across the weak passages, Petrus sweeps his tail over them nonchalantly, Ocha meows insistently, and I chew on the guilty page. With the tender guidance of our contortions, her attention is aroused and focused, she rereads confidently and efficiently, and the miracle occurs: she crushes the doubt that tormented her all night long. "You have to do things seriously, without taking yourself seriously," she told me one day after a particularly successful bout of revising. I had a good laugh, I tell you. If she only knew that she owes her satisfaction to the fact that we take her work very seriously!

Unfortunately, there is one last affliction, more grievous and complex: denial. Sometimes the writer needs to convince herself that her text can hold water when really, it's full of leaks. And the more she sees it, the more she denies it, because writers are practiced schizophrenics who know very well just what they don't want to know. In these cases, you have to come down hard, so we send in Mizu, with her soul of a commando leader. *À la guerre comme à la guerre*, she said one day when all the usual tactics had failed. She resolved to fart onto the offending lines— yes, Mizu farted noisily onto the paper, leaving a few distinct traces, waving her tail with satisfaction. Our writer screamed. Then, after a moment of holding the sheet of paper at extreme arm's length, rereading the prose that had been graced with the stamp of our major general, she shook her head and murmured, "This is really bad."

If we could have shaken paws to congratulate one another, we would have.

There is one last argument I would like to put forward in defense of our cause. Our writer has yet another unique characteristic: she is obsessive, but in a rather particular way. She is obsessed with *lines*. Not the lines in the text: visual lines. Consequently, everything in our home is arranged in such a way as to meet the viewer's gaze with equilibrium: the furniture, the paintings on the wall, the books on the coffee table, the items on the mantelpiece, and even the logs in the log rack (god forfend they actually be used to make a fire). You should see the quarrels she has with her musician because he didn't put a poor (orange) cushion back where it belongs on the (gray) sofa. On her work table, everything is arranged down to the last millimeter: her notebooks, the lamp, the little Japanese vase with its two roses or three hellebores, the primitive plaster cast of Venus, the pens (one white, one black, one red). She is equally obsessive when it comes to her text, and I suspect she drives the typographers at her publishing house crazy. It's a sort of perfectionist compulsion, a delirium of visual control, a pathological love for the finishing touch that has compelled her to hang sublime calligraphy scrolls on the walls, where you will notice

that every line is perfectly equidistant from the others. When people express their surprise at such unhealthy perfectionism, our writer smiles. And one evening she said to me, "Kirinette, beauty and harmony are our only roots in a world that is adrift."

I must say that despite my grievances, I was honored that she chose me as her confidant.

Well, as far as visual harmony or beauty goes, we provide her in her everyday life with ample amounts of it, and then some. What's more, we add movement. We are flawless lines traveling through space, we are moving calligraphy, always changing, always sublime. Our very aspect, our elastic beauty, our pleasing curves make of us a living art, the organic stuff of inspiration: a vector of beauty making its way through this imperfect world, leaving in its wake a perfume of perfection (and a whiff of Japan).

What's more, we always arrange things in such a way that she will find her study in impeccable working order when she arrives at dawn, disheveled and in her pajamas, her fierce gaze inspecting the disposition of every notebook, the alignment of every pen, something we have meticulously verified during the night (in the evening she can't always think very clearly and sometimes she mixes up the black notebook and the red pen). Yes, we are—in all modesty—decorative, tutelary deities watching over the continuity of her rigid little esthetic world, and we make it possible for her to produce texts where, invariably, there will be reference to sublime calligraphy.

From all this, we have come to the obvious conclusion: we are being exploited, with no compensation other than three bowls of kibble a day and a few distracted caresses. Is anyone aware of our contribution to our mistress's labors? Of our kindness, our expertise? Of our close, personal understanding of her inner struggles? Of the inspiration we provide her with? In this world that is adrift, we are the hard sand on which she lays the foundations of her house of words.

So. There can be no more shilly-shallying of whiskers: all work deserves a wage, and we demand our share of the royalties that periodically land in our writer's bank account. With a contract, duly negotiated percentages, social security contributions, and the particulars of a bank account. With our names above the designation "the aforementioned literary advisors" and our signatures 🐾 🐾 🐾 🐾 at the bottom of the contract. "What is the point of cats receiving royalties?" you might (legitimately) inquire. "What does it matter," I am tempted to reply. It's not the thing in itself that is important, it's the symbolic value. Recognition for the people in the shadows; a light shone on the invisible creatures who make the world a better place. We cannot live in a country that had a Revolution yet go on to ignore the labor of more modest folk.

Thus, we wanted to write this book to denounce our working conditions and make our cause known to the wider world. "How did we write it," you might wonder, curious. "With our hearts," is what I am tempted to reply. But I have to confess that we didn't write it ourselves. One evening this winter our writer acted all mysterious and said to me, "Sweetie, you have no idea how much I know." During the night we read the pages she had left on her desk. Pages entitled: The Writer's Cats. And a conclusion: We all liked the text. "Well, fancy that," said Mizu, and this was the first time I've ever seen her look so baffled. Petrus, on the other hand, gave a sneeze of surprise then said, "I like irises better than roses," and Ocha muttered, "Rancid old kibble, what rubbish." As for me, I felt quite proud: she'd picked me to be her narrator, after all. So then we all looked at each other, quite puzzled. It took us a moment to digest the whole thing. But in the end, what matters is that we all agreed.

We all liked the text.

Still, I would like to have the last word. "Otherwise, what would be the point of the whole enterprise," I can hear you say (quite pertinently). If the world is adrift, if humanity is old and disenchanted, if the apocalypse is nigh, if beauty and poetry are the only possible forms of resistance (as our writer has proclaimed in her novels), then we are not simply her literary advisors and protective totems. We are the rampart. We are the shield. Through the intrinsic poetry of our feline existence, we are innocence and harmony preserved, a source of enduring enchantment in spite of catastrophes, and (dare I) artlessness in the face of darkness. Consequently, in addition to royalties, I demand that we be allowed to pose with her as equals, for the posterity of Chartreux workers, and as a tribute to all those who would grace the world with the candid poem of their kindly whiskers.

Printed in Italy, at Puntoweb